TIME FOR
BED'S STORY

Monica Arnaldo

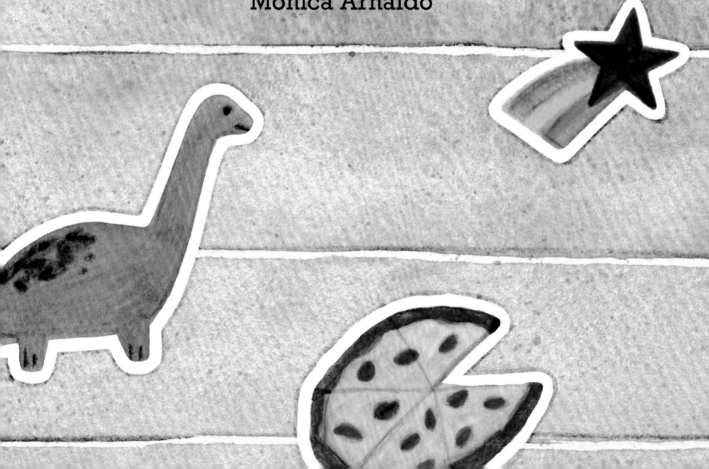

For the Crisdales: fast friends, loyal readers and bedtime champions — MA

Kids Can Press gratefully acknowledges the financial support of the Government of Ontario, through Ontario Creates; the Ontario Arts Council; the Canada Council for the Arts; and the Government of Canada for our publishing activity.

Published in Canada and the U.S. by Kids Can Press Ltd.
25 Dockside Drive, Toronto, ON M5A 0B5

Kids Can Press is a Corus Entertainment Inc. company

www.kidscanpress.com

The artwork in this book was rendered in watercolor.
The text is set in Rockwell.

Edited by Jennifer Stokes
Designed by Barb Kelly

Printed and bound in Shenzhen, China, in 4/2020
by C & C Offset

CM 20 0 9 8 7 6 5 4 3 2 1

Library and Archives Canada Cataloguing in Publication

Title: Time for bed's story / Monica Arnaldo.
Names: Arnaldo, Monica, author, illustrator.
Identifiers: Canadiana 20190201606 | ISBN 9781525302398 (hardcover)
Subjects: LCGFT: Picture books.
Classification: LCC PS8601.R6453 T56 2020 |
DDC jC813/.6 — dc23

TIME FOR BED'S STORY

Monica Arnaldo

Kids Can Press

Hello. Bed here.

Yes, Bed.

Bed has something to say.

Bed knows you do not like bedtime.

Bed hears you say
you are **not** sleepy,

you want five
    more
        minutes,

you **need** a
drink of water.

And Bed gets it.
    But look ...

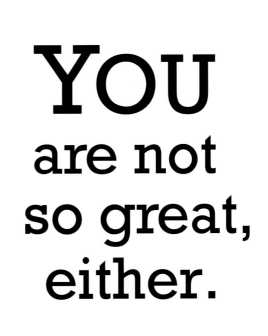

YOU
are not
so great,
either.

First, the **kicking**.

Did you know you kick in your sleep?

Because you do, and it is **a lot**.

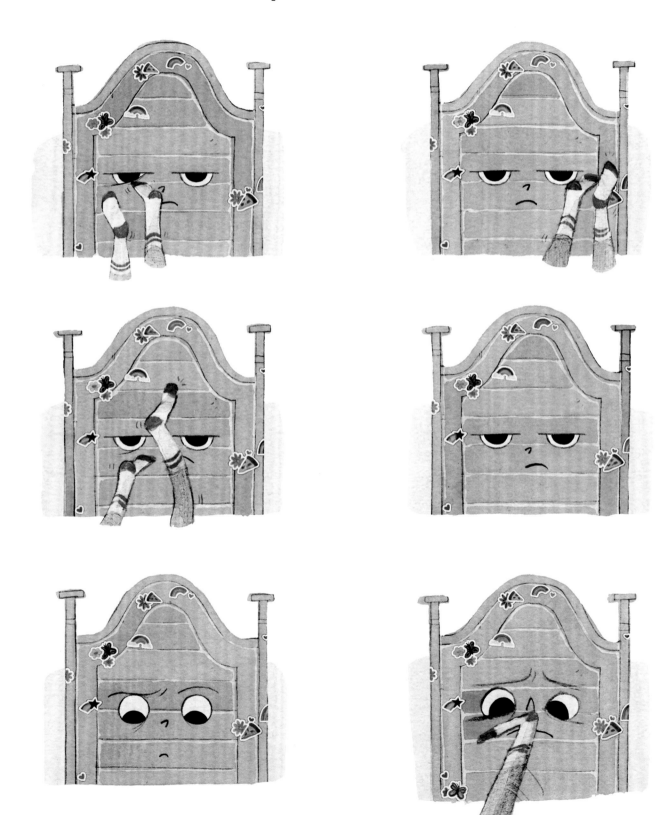

Then there is the **drooling**.

It is wet and cold and also stinky.
Bed hears you *say* you brush your teeth,
but Bed is not so sure.

Also, you take all of Bed's blankets.

Some nights, Bed gets hardly
any sleep at all.

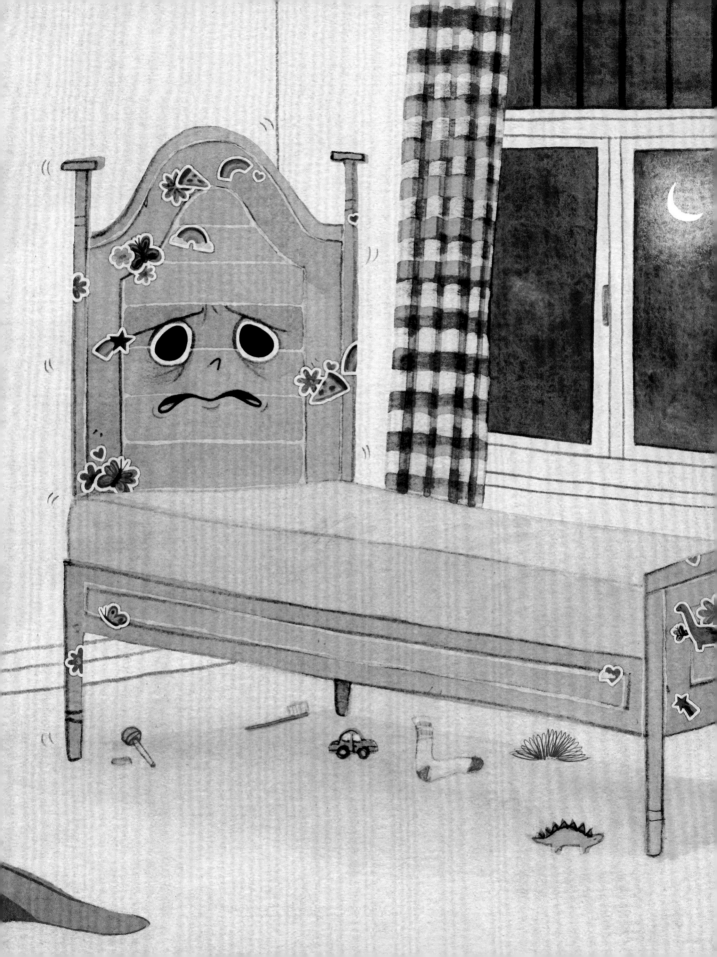

In the daytime, too,
things for Bed are not ideal.

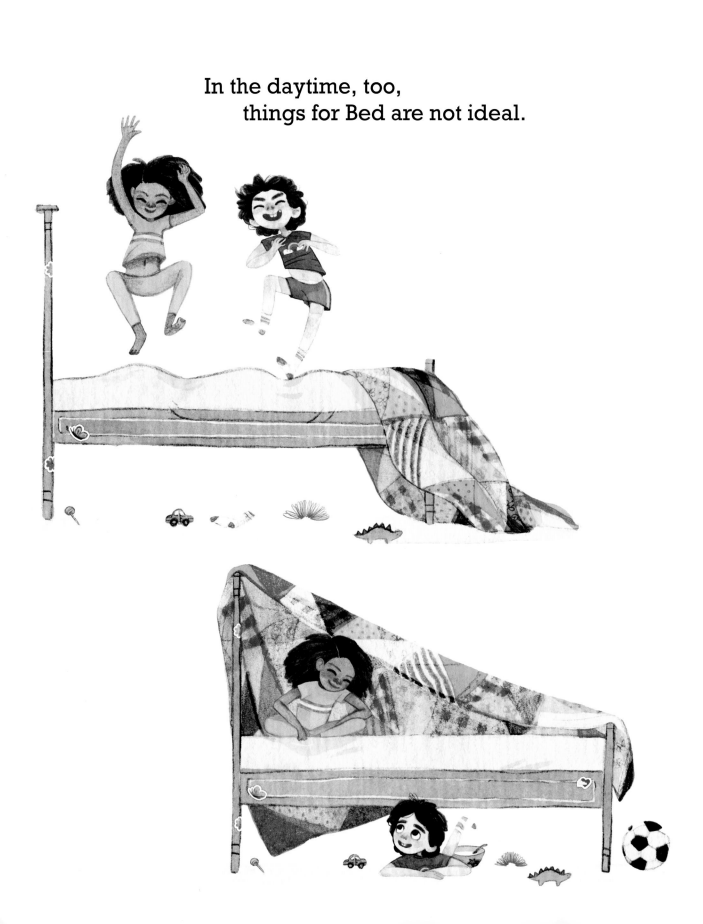

Maybe sometimes you could try a quiet activity ...

like reading.

No. Not like that.

Bed wonders if you notice the smell.

Bed cannot say for sure what is causing it, but Bed has some theories.

Can Bed ask about the stickers?

It seems like Bed is always finding strange things where they should not be.

Worst of all was the tooth.

But does Bed complain?

No. **Never.**

Not one time.

But Bed sees you
are growing up.

Bed thinks maybe now
you can be reasoned with.

So Bed is asking you …
next bedtime, could you possibly,
please, try to think of Bed's feelings also?

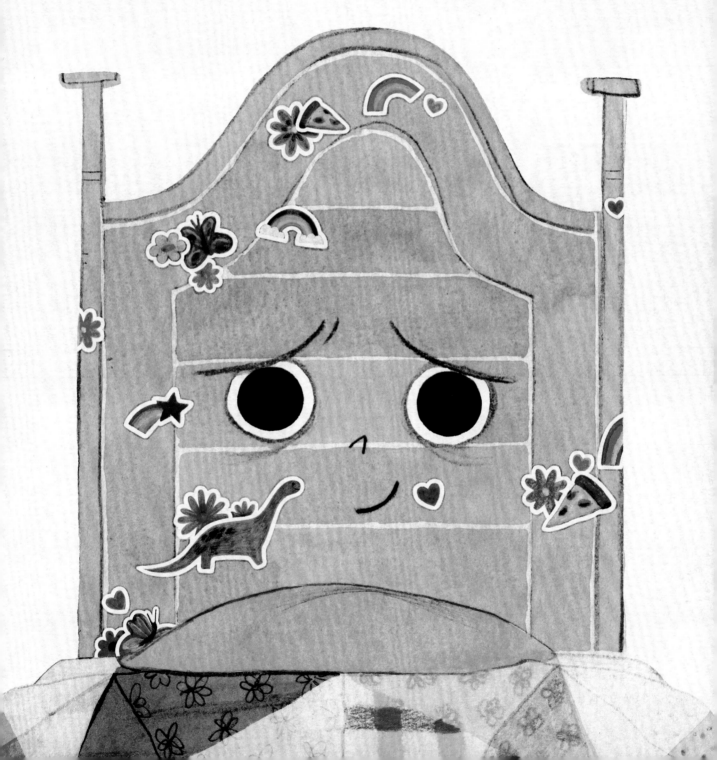

No?

Okay.
Next time, maybe.